RENA MARTHALER

MAGIC

THE CREST

This book is available at Amazon.com, CreateSpace.com, and by contacting the author at magicthecrest@gmail.com.

ISBN-13: 978-1494311001
ISBN-10: 1494311003

Dedicated to my mom, who ROCKS!!!

For Rachel B.

With special thanks to Greta L., Cate S., and Lena W., my BFFs.

And more thank yous—

To my Dad, who is awesome. And my BFF Maya S. And my teachers, Vickie, Dirk, Miss B., Ms. H., Mrs. C., and Mrs. C. And of course, NaNoWriMo.

TABLE OF CONTENTS

MAGIC

THE CREST

CHAPTER ONE I HAVE POWERS AND A SWORD

A bunch of weird things have been beginning to happen since I moved to my new school. I've made like three friends, so things like that are going fine. But I've been having weird dreams and stuff. And, wait, wait, wait, wait, WAIT! Sorry, I should start from the beginning.

I am a ten-year-old girl named Rachel. I just moved to school in New York. (Though I never knew that one of my best friends would soon talk to a chipmunk.) I have three friends named Lily, Ashley, and Zoe. So, we liked to play this game where we all had powers of our own element like fire, storm, ice,

1

and earth - that kind of stuff. Zoe would be ice; Ashley and Lily would be earth (except Ashley was our trainer, and she was at the highest rank). And I would be storm. And also, we would have weapons, like for combat.

But that wasn't even the start. We would fight monsters, I had my own lab, and Ashley and I would pretend that we sometimes accidently turned into something evil called the riddles that would recite prophecy and stuff. I'm starting to bore you, aren't I? Well, suck it up. It's about to get interesting.

So Ashley, Zoe, Lily, and I were just playing that game when this huge clap of thunder (or so I thought) interrupted everything.

"That's weird," said Ashley. "The sky is completely clear." I looked up and saw that she was right.

"Maybe it was you, Rachel," Lily joked.

"Shut up," I scowled. BOOM! We heard it again. I was starting to panic. I could see that the others were, too.

"Guys, seriously, I think that something's happening…" BOOM! Zoe was cut off. Everybody on the field was starting to get really scared. The kindergarteners cried. Even the teachers were really nervous. Then we heard cawing. We all looked up. There was a crow circling above us.

"There's a sonic boom going on somewhere and you guys are distracted by a crow?" Lily cried.

"No, it's holding something," I said. Well, the crow dropped that 'thing' and that 'thing' fell on my face. "It's a note!" I exclaimed. "It says, *Use the locket, watch out for its heads, and good luck.*" I clutched my locket.

"Its *heads*? What does *that* mean?" cried Zoe. Then we heard another boom, and a screech, and the school set on fire.

There were sounds of screaming everywhere. A teacher passed out. (That teacher was a boy.) And then we saw it.

A giant (and I mean GIANT) dragon circled the school spitting acid and fire. We stood there frozen.

The words rang in my ears, *Use the locket*. I ripped my locket off my neck.

"What are you doing?" cried Ashley. The others were still frozen with fear.

I can't believe I am going to do this, I thought. I pried the locket open. It immediately turned into a bronze sword. I screamed and dropped it. Then I realized that the sword was supposed to help me. I picked it up. The dragon screeched again.

"Rachel, what are you holding?" Ashley yelped. "Oh, no. Don't. I'm serious—Rachel." The dragon came closer.

Then another note fell on my face. It read, *Use one of the spells you learned in your games*. Without thinking, I charged.

Things went wrong immediately. I got ready to stab that stupid (what is it, a reptile, amphibian?) ~~butt~~ but it dodged my attack. I got around it somehow, and cut its head off.

And I felt pretty satisfied, but *noooooooo*! It had to grow three more heads in replacement! I cursed.

"Rachel, it's a Hydra!" Ashley yelled. *Are those even real?* I wondered. The Hydra spit some acid. That will do some damage to our school field.

I dodged the acid. Then I thought of the second note. *Use a spell.* I knew it was crazy, but I tried one of the hand motions that Ashley taught me.

I tried one called *Bare Bones*. It was supposed to be a powerful one. Believe it or not, a black stream of magic came bursting out of my fist.

I held the spell until I couldn't hold it anymore. The dragon disintegrated, and I staggered backward and fell on my butt. Then I realized that everyone was staring at me. I started running and signaled for my friends to follow.

We stopped in front of a tree. I seated myself and stared at my hands. My friends stared at me in awe. "How did you do that?" asked Zoe with amazement.

"I don't know. Why don't you try?" I snapped.

She tried one, called *Frostbite*, and froze the ground like an ice skating rink. She screamed.

I stared at her. "See, I'm not the only one with powers!" I said.

"Hey, what about us?" Ashley and Lily complained.

"Go ahead," I urged. Lily did a spell, and a huge chunk of earth formed a circle in front of her. She grinned with pleasure. Ashley concentrated real hard, and two deer came up to her and bowed, and a squirrel offered his nut to her. She smiled real big.

"How come we never did this before?" Zoe wondered out loud.

"Who cares? It's cooler that we got the powers now," I responded.

That night, I had weird dream about that dragon, except this time it talked to me. *To one of the tallest, you will go, to save the smallest, I give you hope. The tallest is very hot, if you don't succeed, she will rot.* "That sounds like a prophecy!" I thought. Then I woke up. We were still under the tree, and the others were still asleep.

"Wake up," I said softly. They sat up and rubbed their eyes. Lily had bed-head. I snickered. Zoe noticed it and also started giggling. The same thing happened to Ashley.

"What?" demanded Lily sleepily.

"Last night I had the weirdest dream, where you had a sword and we could do magic!" yawned Zoe. She noticed the frozen ground where my sword lay. "Aw, man!" she said.

Another note fell on my head. (I think these notes are out to get me.) It read, *To one of the tallest, you will go, to save the smallest, I give you hope. The tallest is very hot, if you don't succeed, she will rot.*

That's the same prophecy that was in my dream! I thought. "Uh, you guys? Look at this note." They came closer to read it.

"You guys thinking what I'm thinking?" asked Zoe.

"Yup. We're going to Oregon!" I replied.

The plane ride was really long. Somehow we convinced our parents to buy us plane tickets. I think they thought that we were on this 'special girl trip' or something. They were probably like, *Bye kids! See you in a month or two!*

When we arrived, we started our trip. We weren't going to stay at a hotel, because it would be too far from our destination. So we brought tents and stuff. As we started to walk, Zoe said, "Rachel, where are we going?"

"I think we are going to the volcano, Mt. Hood," I replied. We kept walking. OMG this walk was getting so boring! Anyway, at noon we set up camp. We were just falling to sleep when we heard this terrible screech. We looked up. Hovering above us was something that looked something like a cross between a lion and an eagle.

"Griffin!" Zoe screamed.

It in fact was a griffin. I stared in horror as the griffin dove down and snatched up Zoe. She screamed with panic and her arms flailed while trying to break free.

I shook Ashley and Lily awake. They sat up drowsily. "What?" they both said lazily. I pointed up. "Oh, derp. Oh derp, oh derp, oh derp!" they cried.

I pulled out my sword. "Use an earth spell!" I shouted. It was kinda hard to talk over the screeching of what, fifty griffins?

The ground shook. Ashley and Lily rose from the ground, a gleaming gold ball encircling them. I stared in shock.

A griffin dove at me. I turned too late. The griffin slashed my shoulder. I fell on my knees, my shoulder searing with pain.

"Rachel!" Zoe screamed somewhere way high up. I made thumbs up and struggled to my feet. I pulled out my sword. One by one, I vaporized the griffins as they dove and sliced their claws through the air at me.

Finally, I had finished all of them. Except one, the one that was holding Zoe. I lunged at her. But Ashley and Lily were still in that gold ball.

The gold ball moved toward Zoe, and then popped. I should've been running at them, but I just stared in horror. I thought they were going to fall! But they didn't. As it seemed, a huge mound of earth rose to catch them, probably at their will.

They both shot a blast of earth ball at the griffin and knocked it out. Zoe fell, but I somehow summoned a cloud to catch her.

The cloud lowered. We rushed toward her. "You guys are awesome!" she said, breathing heavily.

"Yeah well…" Ashley started to say.

"Whoop! Griffins up!" Lily yelped. Zoe jumped up, grabbed her bracelet, pulled it as far as it could go, and it turned into a bow and arrow.

She knocked out an arrow. The griffin vaporized and we just stared. "Cool!" we said.

"Never mind that," she replied. "Your shoulder!"

"It's nothing." I murmured. "Let's keep going."

So we went on. "Hey," said Zoe, "What are those words on your sword?"

"What?"

"There are words on your sword, on the bottom."

"There are?"

"Yeah, what do they say?"

I looked at the bottom. There were indeed words. I squinted. "They say *Black Blade*," I exclaimed.

"Cool!" said Ashley excitedly. "Do we have super cool weapons with awesome names?"

"Hey, I want to figure out what my bow and arrow's name is," said Zoe. She examined her bow. "Nothing," she said with a frown. I looked up at the sky. It was getting dark.

"We better get going," I told them. We moved on through a forest and set up camp under a tree. The next morning we set out on our journey again.

"You guys, I'm hungry," Lily groaned.

"Okay, we'll get some food," I replied.

We stopped at a restaurant in the middle of nowhere. "This place is creepy," said Ashley. It was very creepy. The door creaked when we opened it.

"Hello?" I called.

We stepped inside. There was no one there.

"Hello?" I called again. "You guys, this place *is* creepy. We should leave."

"Hello, there!" said a new voice. "Welcome to Irina's. I am Irina." A skinny woman with short purple hair was leaning at the entrance to the kitchen. "May I help you?"

We stared for a moment. And then Ashley spoke up. "Uh, hi. Is this a restaurant?"

"Why, yes it is! Please sit. I will get a menu." She showed us a table, and then skipped to the kitchen.

"You guys, this place is weird," said Zoe.

"I don't care. I'm ordering a MEGA pizza," said Lily.

"Me, too!" Ashley and I giggled.

"Okay, I will too," grinned Zoe.

"May I have your order?" Irina appeared out of nowhere. We told her what we wanted. She started walking back to the kitchen, and a long, gray tail came from behind her.

"Guys, did you see that?" I shivered. They nodded.

"I told you!" Zoe hissed.

"Here you go!" Again, Irina appeared out of nowhere and handed us massive pizzas. "Enjoy!" We ate.

"I still think this place is weird," said Zoe.

We finished our pizzas, and I asked for one more for the trip. "But don't you want to eat it here?" Irina asked.

"No, thank you," I replied. "We should get out of here," I whispered. "Thank you, miss." We headed for the door.

"Not so fast," cackled Irina. We turned. Irina was standing just a few yards away from us. Her apron was torn and she seemed to have fangs. We watched in horror as she changed. Her skin shredded into dark purplish scales, which would have been funny, except that her eyes started glowing green, and snakes started sprouting where her hair used to be.

"M-Medusa?" Zoe shivered.

Irina hissed. Her snake hair looked offended.

"*Medusa?* No, I am one of her sisters, a Gorgon. Medusa is always the most famous and well known.

13

No one ever knows about Gorgons." Her snakes snapped at each other. "Well, I will show her. I have been trapped here, waiting for Magics and mortals to eat."

I reached for my locket.

"Oh, and one more thing—"

I felt around for it. Irina held up my locket, and Zoe's bracelet.

"Oops, no weapons," she cackled.

"Seriously?" we complained. "You don't know what we are capable of."

"You—try too hard. You will not win!"

"Oh, yes we will!" Together, we charged.

Bad idea. First of all, we had no idea what we were doing. Second, we didn't have weapons. Third, we were all going so fast that we didn't have time to cast a spell. Pretty stupid, huh? Well, the Gorgon didn't move. But, when we almost got to her, she moved out of the way and we smashed into the wall. It was unpleasant.

I looked at Zoe. She nodded and looked at Lily. Lily nodded and looked at Ashley. Ashley nodded and looked at all of us. I hand-motioned *One*, *two*, and *three*. We cast our spells.

I cast *Bare Bones* again. Zoe cast *Octice*. Lily cast *Cat Claw*s and Ashley cast *Earth Struck*. They all hit Irina at the same time. She disintegrated.

I spoke up. "That was too easy. Be prepared for more." We waited.

"Okay we're good!" said Lily cheerfully. "Let's get out of here."

That night, we set up camp. We gazed at the Mount Rushmore. Wait, there isn't a Mount Rushmore in Oregon! "You guys, we're in South Dakota!" said Ashley.

"Dang! Another plane ride!" Lily mumbled.

"Tomorrow," I reminded her. We went back to sleep.

The next day we set off again. When we arrived at the airport, we realized that we didn't have any money to pay for the trip. "Shoot!" said Ashley. She set her head against a wall with an old dirty sign above it. "We almost... hey, what does that sign say?"

15

"It says *Store Room*," I said.

"No, it says, *Moog Gloom*," said Lily.

"No, you dummies, it says, *Magic Loom*!" exclaimed Zoe.

"Oh, that explains the magic mist coming out of it," pondered Lily aloud.

"What?"

"Never mind. Let's go in." Ashley started to walk through the door.

Zoe pulled her back. "I will tell you this: *NO*."

"Oh, give me a break. It will be fun," whined Ashley.

"Let's go in. We should check it out," I said.

"Well, okay," conceded Zoe. We walked through the door.

"How come she listens to you?" Ashley asked. I shrugged. Suddenly Zoe stopped.

"What?" I asked.

She frowned. "There's another door."

"So? Go through it."

"Okay…." She walked through the door. Behind it was another door. Behind that one was

16

another one. Then we went through like five more doors until we came to a room. The room was a wide-open space, and it had three people in it. But the thing that really made us gasp was the thing in the middle.

A huge machine sat in the center of the room. It was made of glass tubes with neon green liquid working its way down them. A couple other tubes had blue and purple liquids. But that's not the point. All the liquids were going down through filters and stuff, and heading towards a giant loom placed at the bottom.

I guessed it was the Magic Loom. It seemed to be making lots of silver thread with sparkling mist around it, filling the room with lavender scent. It made you want to sit down and watch it, but I forced myself not to. I snapped at myself for getting distracted.

"What is that?" quivered Zoe.

"That is the Magic Loom," said a voice.

CHAPTER TWO KAYLA

Standing in front of us was a tall woman with short black hair. She wore a white lab coat and black boots. She held a clipboard and had a pencil on her ear.

"Uh, sorry we came, we'll go now," said Zoe nervously.

The women protested. "Oh no, don't go. I like visitors. My two friends here are my assistants." The two people standing behind her smiled and waved.

"Are you Magics searching for a ride?" We nodded. "Well then, come right up. I will show you how to get where you want to go."

"The Magic Loom produces silver thread that contains potions for travel. The blue one is a map potion, the purple one is a time potion, and the green one is a teleportation potion. To go somewhere, all you need to do is cut some thread, tie it around your waist, and think about where you want to go."

"For a group," she gestured at us, "you bunch up, tie it around all of you, and you all think about where you want to go," she explained. Then she warned us, "But do not think of different places than one another. For if you do, you will all cease to exist." Then she changed to cheerful mode. "Got it?" We nodded.

"Are there Magic Looms at every airport?" asked Lily.

"Oh, yes. We are all over the world."

"Cool!"

"Yes, it is very cool. Now let me tie you up."

"For free?" I asked. She nodded and cut some string. "Okay, everybody," I said as she started to tie the string to us. "Think about Oregon in *one...*" She secured the string, "*two*," she stepped back, "*three!*" Everything blurred and my vision went dark.

My first feeling when I woke up was landing on my butt. Not very pleasant.

"Ow," Ashley groaned.

"We are in Oregon!" Lily announced.

"Okay, let's go to the volcano." Zoe sat up, rubbing her head. "I've been wanting to ask," she said, "Who is '*the smallest*'?" We shrugged.

"Beats me. Let's just find this kid," I said.

We walked on. We were just getting bored when we heard a scream. "AHHH! NOT AGAIN!" I screamed. "NO MORE MONSTERS!!!"

"Rachel, really," said Ashley calmly.

I relaxed. "Anyway, let's see what this is about." We turned around. And climbed over rocks. And ducked through bushes. And climbed boulders.

Finally, after like five miles, we came to a stop. "That was really loud screaming," puffed Lily.

Zoe raised a shaky finger and pointed. "I think we're where we want to go," she said.

She was right. Across from us was the huge Mt. Hood. We were literally at the base of the mountain, and I was fine with that.

"We're here," said Ashley softly. "Let's wait for any letters to guide us." We waited.

I sighed. "Nothing. Let's go."

We started up the mountain. An hour later, a crow circled above us.

We waited. The crow dropped the note, and this time I caught it. I was used to these notes. I read it. "You guys, it says, *Fire element, you will seek, to find the girl, you will speak.*"

"Okay, I don't understand much, but I think we have to find a girl," said Zoe.

"Good, so we know it's not a boy," joked Lily.

"I get it," I said, looking up from the paper. Then I looked up at the sky. "YA' HEAR THAT? YOUR STUPID PROPHECIES ARE TOO CLEAR! THINK ABOUT IT BEFORE YOU DROP IT!!!" Then I mumbled, "Not like those awesome ones in Percy Jackson."

21

Zoe glared at me. "Anyway, we know it's a girl. And I think she's a Magic, too." We nodded. "So we have to find her." We nodded again. "Don't you get it?" she cried. "We have to go! Now!" She wagged her finger at the top of the mountain. We nodded. She sighed, "Come on. Let's go to the top of this stinking old mountain." She started walking up and we followed.

Halfway up we stopped for pizzas and camped out for the night. "BIG mountain," sighed Lily. We went to sleep.

The next morning we set off. Again. About three quarters of the way up the hill, we looked back to check on Ashley. She seemed to be falling behind. But when we looked back, she wasn't there. We scanned around us, up the hill, and then we looked up at the sky.

Ashley was screaming and flailing her arms frantically. A Fury was holding her. The Fury was ugly. I looked at the others and we nodded.

"A little help?" Ashley screamed. We nodded again. Then we all closed our eyes, concentrated, and pushed with our hands.

Chunks of earth burst out of Lily's hand. Sparkling ice came streaming out of Zoe's palm. And then blue lightning shot out of my fist. They all hit the Fury at once. It twitched and flinched in pain, but stayed in the air and held Ashley fast. Eventually, even though the Fury was getting weaker, Lily and I fell to the ground, exhausted.

That meant it was up to Zoe. She held it up, pouring all of her strength into her spell. But it was too much for the Fury. It started to freeze over.

We watched in horror as the Fury froze like an ice cube and fell to the ground, where it shattered. Ashley fell with it. I summoned a cloud to catch her. Then we rushed over to Zoe.

"That was amazing!" said Ashley. Zoe fell over. Ashley winced.

"Let's rest," I said. We laid out our sleeping bags and climbed into them. Another note fell. It read, *Tick tock*. I took a pen out of my bag, and wrote, *Seriously?* Then I threw it back up.

A moment later it came back down and this time it read, *Just kidding*. I crumpled the note and went back to sleep.

The next day, we ate the last of the food and set out. Up, I mean. It was a very short trip. We didn't realize how close we were to the top.

"Well, we're here, at the top. What do we do now?" asked Lily.

I replied, "Set up camp and find food."

So that's what we did. Zoe and I laid out the sleeping bags and stuff, while Lily and Ashley went to find food. They came back grinning, with pizza and sodas in their hands. We sat down to eat. "Yummy, yummy, yummy!" said Lily with a mouthful of pizza.

"Where in the world did you find pizza and sodas on Mt. Hood?" I asked. Ashley and Lily shrugged.

When we finished, we got serious. "So, we're supposed to find a girl of the fire element," I started.

24

Then, as if on cue, we heard faint crying. We rushed towards the sound. It seemed to be coming from behind a tree. We looked on the other side of it.

On the other side was a girl, about one year younger than us. She had curly brown hair down to her shoulders, and she was wearing tattered clothes. She looked up at us.

"W-who are you?" she asked with a shaky voice.

"Um, Magics," said Zoe soothingly.

"You have powers? I do."

We nodded. "What's your name?" Zoe asked.

"Kayla. What's yours?"

We introduced ourselves. "You'd better come with us," I said. We helped her up and started our way down the mountain.

I caught another note. It read, *Good job*. I wrote back, *I know*, and sent it back up. And that's how Kayla joined our group.

On the way down, Kayla asked, "Do you think you will have any other quests, like with me?"

I shrugged, "No idea. But you have joined our team, and you're not getting away. Let's get cleaned up."

When we got to the bottom, we found a hotel and reserved it for six days. We plopped down in our room. We all fell on our beds, exhausted. It felt so comfortable being in a heated room, with real comfy beds, a TV, books. We hadn't had those in a really long time.

"Comfy, so soft and comfy," said Lily, her face buried in bed sheets. Then we all fell asleep except for me. I lay awake, wondering what our next quest would be. But eventually, I fell asleep.

The next morning, we were ready to leave. We packed up, went to the airport, got some food, and showed Kayla how to use the Magic Loom. When we got to New York, we walked home together, because we all lived in the same apartment building.

Suddenly I stopped. "Uh, guys? I think we have a problem," I said nervously. "Where is Kayla going to live?" We all looked at the ground.

For a really long time nothing happened. But then, Lily sprang up. "I HAVE AN IDEA!!!" she shouted right into Zoe's ear. "We can trade off. First, Kayla will live at your house," she pointed at Zoe. "Then at your house, Ashley. Then, at Rachel's house, then at mine!" She giggled. And then we can all have a campout together, once a week!"

We thought it was a great idea, but I spotted a problem. "Where the heck are we going to find a forest in New York?" I asked.

Lily replied, "We're going to California, of course!"

"How are we going to get there?"

"The fastest transportation!"

"An airplane?"

She giggled. "No, silly, did you really forget? The Magic Loom!" I slapped myself for being so stupid.

"So, see you tomorrow?" I asked.

"Yep," they replied. We walked up the stairs, stopped at the first floor to drop Zoe and Kayla off, and continued up. On the second floor, we dropped

27

off Ashley. Lily and I walked on. Our rooms were on the top two floors.

"Do you think we will get any more quests?" asked Lily. I shrugged. Fifth floor, sixth, seventh, eighth, ninth, tenth, eleventh, twelfth, we stopped at thirteen.

"You know," said Lily as she started walking through the door, "I kinda thought of the campout together as a meeting, you know what I mean? Like we can swap news about crow messages and stuff. Anyway, see ya." She walked away.

Then I walked up to the top floor, walked into my room, and fell asleep immediately. The next morning was Sunday. I had to pack for our camping trip. I packed, well, you would know.

Anyway, I ate breakfast early so my mom wouldn't know that I came back, and went to get the others. They were waiting at their doors. "Ready?" I asked. They nodded. We were all very excited. Especially Kayla.

"I can't believe it!" she said. "My first trip with you guys!"

"Okay," I said. "Let's go to California!"

When we got there we saw a sign that said *Sierra Nevada Mountains.* I guessed that was what this place was called. We started our way up Devil's Peak. When we got to the top, we set up camp. Lily and Ashley made little chairs around a pit that they made out of earth. Kayla made fire/magic for our warmth, Zoe froze some sodas, and I electrified an old broken radio and made it work. (I did that with all electric things.)

Then we sat down to cook and eat our food. "So," asked Zoe. "Any news?"

Kayla raised her hand. "I got a crow message last night," she said. We all stared at her. "I brought it. Come see."

We crowded around her. I read it aloud.

"It says, '*Since this is your second quest, you will find the one who bears the crest. You will help her find the crown jewel. You will use your only tool.*'"

"Holy hot dogs."

"What is it?" asked Kayla.

"It's... nothing."

29

"I think we have another quest," said Lily cheerfully.

"Great!" said Ashley. "Let's go to sleep now." So we climbed into our sleeping bags and fell fast asleep. The next morning we went to the airport and got into the Magic Loom's silver string.

"Think of the element universe," I said. They all looked at me strangely. "Just do it!" I said.

Our vision went dark. When we opened our eyes, we were on land, but we could see the universe around us. "Yep, we're here," I said. My friends stared at me.

"How did you know?" asked Kayla.

I shrugged. We looked at our surroundings. We could see the universe around us, but it looked as if we were standing on it. In fact, we were. There were planets around us, but we weren't on solid ground. I sighed.

"Welcome to the magic galaxy," I said.

"So where do we start?" asked Kayla eagerly.

I pointed to a planet that was completely covered in ice.

"There."

We walked on air to the planet. I could feel the temperature drop. When we stepped on it, the planet felt like a giant ice cube (that's because it *was* one).

Every step we took was slippery. Although Zoe was in heaven. She climbed ice trees, ate an ice apple, and petted an ice dog.

"You definitely are an ice type," I laughed. She was too busy chasing an ice squirrel to notice me.

Finally, we spotted a town (completely made of ice, of course). It had little shacks for houses, and little creatures lived in them. They were one foot tall, with little tails sticking out of their backs. They had big, round eyes, a little nose, a little mouth, and two big ears.

"Those … are … ADORABLE!" said Zoe. She raced into the town.

"Zoe, wait!" I started to say. But it was too late. She raced into the middle of the square, her eyes darting back and forth.

"Zoe's gone mad," Ashley whispered. I nodded.

All the little creatures gasped when they saw Zoe. Then they started talking to each other in some kind of cute gibberish. Then they seemed to agree on something, and then they bowed down to Zoe. A few of them fell over.

She just stood there, shocked. The creatures beckoned her forward, and we followed. They led us inside a giant castle, where they showed us a photo of a girl that looked a lot like Zoe. Same light blonde hair, same icy blue eyes and kind smile. Then they showed us to a giant throne room.

It was completely made of ice, obviously. The throne was beautiful, though. The creatures waddled to a cupboard, and then brought out a sign that said, *Wee aw da Pippins!*

Then they brought out something else. They waddled over to us and knelt in front of Zoe with a pillow in their little hands. On the pillow was a crown, an icy crown, with little crystal dangly things hanging off of it. In the middle was a diamond. The Pippins asked Zoe to sit down. They put the crown on her head.

"Zoe?" I asked.

She was too shocked to speak. Lily went in front of Zoe and stuck out her tongue. Kayla clapped really heavy books together in front of her face. Nothing. Ashley stomped around on the floor. I reflected light on her face. Nada. Then the Pippins brought out a little bottle of vanilla and held it in front of her nose.

Zoe breathed in, and sighed, "I love vanilla."

The Pippins smiled. They asked her to stay.

"No, I'm sorry. I am on a quest with my friends. But I will come back and check on you."

The Pippins looked disappointed. But they seemed happy again when they saw Zoe's smile. Then we said goodbye, walked out of the castle, and started walking on air, into space.

Zoe was examining her crown. "Hey guys, do you think this is the crown jewel?" she asked. We shook our heads. She put her crown away.

"Let's focus on finding Moonstr...." My voice wavered. My friends looked at me oddly.

We walked till we saw a fiery planet. It was literally on fire. "Let's go there!" said Kayla. So we walked there.

When we got there, my feet were on fire, so Kayla had to put a protection spell on them. We walked to a village, and on the way, just like Zoe, Kayla went crazy. She zipped from burning trees to lava rivers. It looked pretty amazing.

We entered a village, but this time no one was there. We searched everywhere until we heard a little *meow*. We followed the sound.

We came to a little cat. The cat was on fire, and it seemed like it wanted us to follow him. So we did. Kayla was jumping up and down.

We arrived at a flaming castle. The cat led us to a throne room, and then meowed a really long meow. It was really loud. We covered our ears. The windows shattered, and then burst into flames.

Right after the meows/screaming, about a dozen more firecats swarmed into the room. They looked at a picture on the wall, then back at Kayla. The picture, Kayla. The picture, Kayla. Then they got out a ladder, climbed to the ceiling, and got out something shiny. When they got down, one of them set down a pillow and pushed it towards Kayla.

Sitting on the pillow was a crown. It was made of flames, but it had a ruby in the middle. Just like at the ice planet, they asked her to stay. But she declined. "I will come and visit, see how you're doing," she said. They seemed happy with that.

She put the crown in her backpack. "Do you think that this is the crown jewel?" she asked.

I replied, "I don't think that's the crown jewel. I don't think that any of the crowns that we have or will get are the crown jewel."

As we walked, we saw a planet that looked just like planet earth, except with no water, and the ground changed before our eyes. "Cool!" Ashley and Lily said. We directed to the planet.

When we stepped on the planet, it felt like the ground was alive. It was weird. All the people that lived on the planet were normal animals, but every kind.

All the animals gasped when they saw Lily and Ashley. A little chipmunk came up to Ashley and chattered in her ear. "He says that…" she started to say.

I interrupted her. "You speak chipmunk?"

She glared at me. "Yes, I do. He says that he needs help. He needs two helpers."

Lily raised her hand. "Oooh, pick me! Pick me!" she said.

"Okay, you're volunteer number one and I'm volunteer number two," Ashley said.

"Whoa, whoa, whoa. You're just gonna volunteer for some dangerous thing?" Zoe asked.

"Nah, it's not dangerous."

"This is going to be dangerous," Ashley whimpered as the chipmunk talked to her. We were following him. We were led to a big underground castle. Ashley translated, "*Volunteer number one.*"

Lily raised her hand. We walked to a wall behind a throne room. Ashley whispered a plan to Lily, while Lily nodded.

Lily walked into a room and we followed. It was a wide, spacious room. And it had a big throne in the middle. Sitting on the throne was a GIANT bear. He was wearing a golden crown and a red king's cape. Lily walked up to him.

"Uh, excuse me?" said Lily.

The bear grunted. He looked up at Lily. He talked in bear language. She translated his growls (sort of). She said, "Dude, *I* dare entering your throne room. And I'm pretty sure that the earth metal is titanium, not gold."

The bear snarled.

"Whoa, watch your language!"

The bear roared back.

"What am I here for? I'm here to go against you."

The bear grunted in surprise.

"Yes, *I* dare challenge the great and mighty you. I challenge you to a duel," Lily smirked.

We stared at her.

"Let the duel begin!" she declared. I thought she had gone mad. Lily saw my face.

"Aw, let it go, Rachel. Against a bear? No problem. Besides, I found out I have this." She took out a little trinket shaped like a heart. There was a button in the middle of it. She pressed the button and the heart trinket turned into a poisonous dagger. We stared at her.

The bear took off his cape and crown and set them down gently. Then he went down on four paws and got ready to pounce. Lily braced herself, dagger in hand. Then, they charged.

Well, the bear charged. Lily just stood there. But right when the bear was about to pounce on her, she moved out of the way and the bear crashed into the wall. I guess she had learned something from Irina. The bear sat up rubbing his head, and then changed to battle mode again.

They fought and fought, the bear losing his strength more and more. Then finally, Lily did something weird and amazing at the same time to end the battle. She called the chipmunk and asked him a favor. The chipmunk came back with like forty chickens following. The chickens started doing the chicken dance.

We all were confused. But it was the bear that looked the most puzzled. He looked at the chickens, completely flustered. I snapped out of it just in time to see Lily sneak up behind the bear. She raised her dagger, but then hesitated. Everybody knew that an earth Magic couldn't kill an animal. Then she raised her dagger again, but this time with the flat side to the bear. Then she whacked him. He crumpled.

Lily poked the bear. He was out cold. The chipmunk and the chickens cheered.

"That was great!" said Ashley. The chipmunk whispered something to her. "Phooey," she said. "By the way guys," Ashley grinned, "the chipmunk's name is Cocoa."

We followed Cocoa all the way up a mountain and on the way we met another chipmunk. "His name is Puffy." Ashley explained. Chipmunks named Puffy and Cocoa? *This has gone too far for cuteness*, I thought. The adorable team led us to the top of the mountain.

We heard a growl and I thought it was just the wind, so I almost walked right into a dragon's cave, but Zoe pulled me back behind a rock. I peered around a corner and saw a giant dragon, its wings as big as mountains. The wings were solid black at the bottom, but you could see that its color was changing from black, to dark blue, to green. It had a sleek black body and horns. It had spikes on its head and tail. It had blue glowing spots all over that resembled its skeletal structure.

"Moonstruck," I growled.

Kayla looked confused. "You know her?" she asked. I nodded.

"It's a girl!" Lily cried. I nodded.

The dragon grunted. She started to fly up a little, and then she came down. Ashley urged the chipmunks to go away, telling them that we could handle this. Kayla pushed me out from behind the rock. I drew my sword, for the dragon was already awake.

"Moonstruck?" I asked. I heard Kayla telling Ashley and Zoe and Lily about how she still doesn't know how I know the dragon's name.

"What are *you* doing here?" the dragon sneered.

"I'm here to ask you something," I replied.

"What might that be?"

"Why are you bothering these little creatures?" I said.

"Me? Bother them?" the dragon laughed. "I've hardly been doing that. Anyway, I needed you to come. By the way, I know your friends are behind that rock. They can come out." My friends slowly crept out from behind the rock. "Good. Now, I believe you are on a quest for me."

"Sort of," I mumbled.

"I heard you. Now, you must know that before we go on the quest, there is something else that we need to do." I rolled my eyes.

"We must find my sister, Silverstream."

I gasped. "Holy hot dogs, is she missing?" I sputtered.

"No, it's just that we need her on this quest," explained Moonstruck.

Moonstruck followed us into the universe. "So, why were you living on the earth planet?" asked Zoe.

"Cause' I chased her there," I muttered under my breath.

"Shut up," Moonstruck said to me. Then she turned to Zoe. "It's a very comfy planet," Moonstruck said politely.

I changed the subject. "So, are we going to the storm planet next?" I asked hopefully.

Moonstruck answered, "Sure. But first I should change form." My friends looked puzzled. Then Moonstruck closed her eyes. A blinding light forced us to look away.

When we looked back, a girl our age stood there instead of the dragon. Dark brown hair tumbled across her shoulders, and she had gray, stormy eyes.

"Moonstruck?" Kayla asked.

Moonstruck nodded. "This will be my form when I go on your quest with you."

"Great," I said.

Suddenly, Lily shouted, "Planet ahoy!" We looked ahead. There was a blue planet, with electricity all around.

"How are we going to get in?" asked Ashley. Moonstruck looked at me.

I sighed. "I'll break the barrier for a while," I said. So I held up the barrier while my friends walked through it. When we stepped on the ground, I realized that all the different sections on this planet were based on different kinds of weather. And right now we were in the...

"—rainy section! It's so rainy!" complained Lily.

We walked all the way to the lightning section. "This is where I last saw Silverstream," said Moonstruck. We walked into a village. The houses weren't houses, they were caves.

"This place is so cool!" I said. Suddenly, a big wolf with electric bolts around it bounded up to me. I totally freaked. But the wolf just sat down and wagged his tail. I touched him. He liked it. I scratched him behind the ear. He liked it. Suddenly, with a poof, he turned into a cute little bogle (a cross between a beagle and a boxer). It was adorable. Then he seemed like he wanted us to follow him. We followed him up to a stormy mountain. There was blue sparkling light swirling around the top. Then I realized where it was coming from.

At the top of the mountain was a big, sleek, perfectly white dragon. *Silverstream*, I thought. She was blowing out the blue light.

"Silverstream!" I cried. She looked down at me. The blue light began to dissolve. The light started to dim and get darker. Then she realized what was happening and started blowing again.

"What is she doing?" I asked Moonstruck.

She replied sadly, "Oh, that's easy. She's holding up the universe."

CHAPTER THREE How To

MAKE A UNIVERSE JEWEL

"We have to go and help her!" I cried.

"There's no use unless one of you is willing to do it for her," Moonstruck sighed. But I didn't care. Silverstream was a kind person (dragon, whatever). I ran up the side of the mountain before they could pull me back.

I was huffing and puffing when I got to the top. Silverstream was huge up close — as big as Moonstruck. "I can't allow you to keep doing that. You don't deserve it," I said.

45

She looked down at me and the sky drooped. She was about to put it back up, but instead I pushed her out of the way and held it up myself. It felt like I was lifting a thousand pounds on my shoulders. The sky was heavier than I thought. I guess I wasn't thinking, which was really stupid on my part. I could feel all my strength leaving me.

Silverstream was shocked. Then she cried out.

As my power was leaving me, I remembered something. I wasn't supposed to hold this up. Neither was Silverstream. I thought this guy named Locious was supposed to (I don't know why, maybe its my *magic instinct*). Just then, as if on cue, I saw a man run across the bottom of the mountain. *Locious*, I thought. Silverstream seemed to notice as well. She growled and charged after the man.

My friends came running up to me. I could hear them whispering, "I bet that's heavy." I thought *duh*, but I couldn't say that out loud. I didn't have enough strength.

Then Kayla did something that really surprised me. Right when I was about to collapse, she pushed me out of the way and started to hold it up herself. I staggered out of the way. But then another weird thing happened. Zoe pushed Kayla out of the way and held it up herself.

I stood there, confused. Then Lily held it up. Then Ashley. Then, surprisingly, Moonstruck. She changed to giant dragon mode and held it up with her horns. I stared in shock. "Don't be so surprised, dummybutt," she growled.

I was shocked. So I also shoved Moonstruck out of the way and took her place. But I didn't have to hold the sky for more than five minutes. Silverstream came bounding up the mountain with a man in her jaws. He struggled to get free.

Silverstream gently pushed me out of the way and put Locious in my place. I collapsed.

"Thank you so much!" I cried to Silverstream. She had changed to human form. She had stormy gray eyes like Moonstruck, but her hair was such a light blond that it resembled white. She smiled.

"Better get on with your quest," she said.

"Aren't you coming?" I asked.

Silverstream laughed. "Of course I am!" she said.

Suddenly, we heard a little *meow*. I don't want this to sound like a mystery show, but it seemed to be coming from Kayla's bag.

We looked inside of the bag. Hidden under Kayla's flame crown was the little cat that guided us through the fire planet. "You came with us?" asked Kayla, surprised. The cat licked her hand.

"She wants to go on the quest with you," translated Lily.

"Well, that's fine with me," replied Kayla happily. "I'm gonna name you Ash." The cat seemed happy with that.

The puppy that had guided us through the storm planet tugged on my shoelace. "He wants to come too," said Ashley.

I giggled. "Yes, you can come too. I'll name you Thunder."

We set out to find a place to shelter for the night, with Lily, Ashley, and Zoe complaining how they didn't get a pet. It was kind of annoying. The fun part was that I managed to get everybody a ride on a cloud.

We rode all the way back to Moonstruck's cave. Lily and Ashley were really happy about that because Puffy and Cocoa came scuttling up to them. Puffy really was happy to see Lily, and Cocoa wanted to be with Ashley. We decided that the chipmunks would come on the quest with us.

That made Zoe's complaining worse, until Lily said, "Surprise!" and gave her a little ice bunny. He was adorable.

"I am gonna name him Snowy!" Zoe said.

Ashley rolled her eyes. "Why am I not surprised about that name?" she said.

Zoe giggled and said, "Because it sort of rhymes with Zoe! I didn't even know there was such thing as an ice bunny! I'm so excited that my voice is going high!"

So we brought our 'pets' on the journey. But first we camped out in Moonstruck's cave (like I said before. Do I have to remind you of everything?).

Kayla made a fire (like always) and we sat around it. "So, what's your quest about?" asked Silverstream.

Moonstruck laughed. "You don't know what it's about? Sister, I thought you were keeping up with modern times," she hooted.

Silverstream glared at her sister. "Well, excuse me. I should have stopped my work of holding up the universe to check my surroundings, while you were in a different world."

They argued back and forth. "Uh, I'd hate to break up your family reunion/fight," said Zoe, stroking Snowy. "But I think we have better things to talk about."

"That's right," Kayla jumped in. "Our quest is to find the crown jewel for you two, so stop fighting. And I have a right to say that," she said with triumph.

Both Silverstream and Moonstruck looked at her. Their expression read, *I can't believe you just said that. To us.*

"You know we can…" Moonstruck started to say.

Lily interrupted her. "Kill us with a snap of your fingers? You should really consider it before you do that."

"I don't…" Moonstruck said.

"Think it's a good idea to be arguing with a universe type Magic, whose original form is a dragon?" Lily finished.

"It's not…"

"Safe to be doing this and you should really shut up."

"How do you…"

"Know exactly what you are about to say? It's what I do, baby."

Okay. That was really weird. I stared at her.

"What?" she said. "I learned how to read people when I was six." Lily seemed happy with that.

To make sure that Moonstruck didn't blast her to a million pieces, I sent Lily to find some food or something. So we waited, and waited, and waited.

"You know," said Ashley. "I have a small feeling that this is getting more boring then it should be," she said. We waited some more.

Finally, Zoe stood up. "It's way too quiet. I am going to check on Lily, whether you're coming or not," she blurted out.

"I'll come," I said, also standing. "Anybody else?" I looked around. Nobody said a word.

Zoe and I crept along the forest. Zoe's bow already had an arrow in it and my sword was ready. It was way too silent for Lily to be here.

Then we saw a glowing green light. We cautiously walked toward it.

As we got closer, the image became clearer. It was a big, glowing, green Yin Yang symbol. Then I saw what I came for.

In front of the green ball of terror stood Lily. Her eyes were glazed and glassy and glowing green like the ball. She wasn't jumping around saying, *Yay! Ying Yang ball thingy!* She was just standing there, completely unlike her.

"Zoe, loo…" I turned to face my friend, but she wasn't there. I looked back at Mr. Yin Yang. Zoe was waking slowly towards the ball, her eyes glazed over just like Lily's.

I almost ran to their aid, but then I stopped. How would I save my friends, and not get possessed by Confuscia?

In my head, I made a plan. It was desperate, but it was all I had.

I concentrated on myself. My image, and any others who look, speak, or act like me. I concentrated on all of the electricity inside of me (and boy, I had a lot). Suddenly, it all shot out of me.

The electricity formed a vertical oval. Then some of it came to the middle and formed a glassy image.

I looked directly at the mirror I just made and saw my own reflection. The mirror made me want to stare at my reflection forever, but I knew my own plan.

I pushed the mirror easily ('cause it was floating) towards the Yin Yang. It was a perfect shot. The mirror went straight in front of the Yin Yang, and even though the symbol didn't have eyes, all of its attention went to its reflection.

That was my chance. I lunged for Lily and Zoe. But I couldn't get them out of the trance.

I shook their shoulders. I waved my hand in front of their face. I slapped them. It didn't work. I sighed. I even dared to look back at the Confuscia. Thunder danced around my feet, and then ran behind a tree.

It was beginning to realize what I was doing. I leapt out of the way just before it saw me.

Okay, I thought, *time for plan B*. But I didn't have a plan B. Like I said, it was a desperate plan, so I didn't have time to think of any others. I needed help. So I did the only choice left.

I ran. I ran and ran all the way back to the campsite.

When I got back, everybody was sitting around the campfire, as if they were waiting for me. "Rachel! We were waiting for you!" said Kayla.

"I need help! Now! Please!" I cried.

They looked at me, puzzled. "With what?" asked Ashley.

"Zoe and Lily!" I exclaimed.

"But they're right here," said Moonstruck. She gestured to two girls sitting next to her that looked exactly like Zoe and Lily. They smiled.

"WHAT?" I blurted out.

Silverstream looked worried. "Show us what you're so fussy about," she said. The girls' smile faded.

I walked to the place where the REAL Zoe and Lily were. They were still standing in front of the Yin Yang, but this time it looked like it was forming a force field around them.

I was glad that Moonstuck and Silverstream made fake Lily, fake Zoe, Ashley, and Kayla come along. Fake Zoe and Lily looked embarrassed.

Moonstruck looked really mad, which was a good thing for us, and a bad thing for fake Zoe and fake Lily. "Who are you?" she demanded. Which sounded really scary from a girl that could turn into a dragon any moment.

They smiled politely. "Why, we're Zoe and Lily," said fake Lily.

Moonstruck looked at me. I shook my head. Then she looked at Ashley. "What do you think?" she asked.

Ashley smiled. "I think they're as real as I am," she said innocently.

Just before I was about to ask if there was something wrong with Ashley, Kayla shouted. "Look! Ashley's possessed too!" she cried. I looked at the Yin Yang again. Sure enough, Ashley was standing in front of the symbol, her eyes glazed and green just like the others.

"Agh! I have never been this stuck! I don't know how to solve this!" I cried.

Moonstruck rolled her eyes. "Dude, can't we just kill the fakes, get the symbol thingy from behind, and then go get some food?" she asked.

I was shocked. Since when did I become so stupid? I could have used that idea in the first place. I nodded. "Let's do this," I said.

Moonstruck attacked fake Zoe, Silverstream attacked fake Lily, and I got fake Ashley (yippee). But, sadly, they had the exact bodies as our friends.

We did that, while Kayla crept up behind the symbol, planning to slice it with my sword. I had borrowed Lily's dagger while she was possessed, so I could fight. I wasn't very good with daggers, but it had to do.

As I was fighting, I could hear taunts coming from fake Lily. "You wouldn't hurt a friend, would you?" she said.

"Okay," muttered Silverstream. "You are so not Lily."

For Moonstruck it was easy. Fake Zoe pulled out her bow and arrow, but she couldn't fire from close range. So she was helpless.

Silverstream knocked fake Lily's dagger out of her hand, and I had a good chance because fake Ashley didn't have a weapon yet. Okay. I admit that I was a little scared of her. She seemed so intimidating in battle mode. "You don't know was I can do!" she snarled.

That's the thing. I didn't know what Ashley could do, so she could come at me with anything.

But then everything started to go wrong. Suddenly, fake Zoe started using her arrows as spears. And whenever one broke, she got out a new one. So then Moonstruck started actually getting hurt. Fake Zoe knocked her off her feet and her head hit the ground.

And fake Lily started using her earth powers. She melted a rock around Silverstream and it went up to her neck. "Whoa. This is so embarrassing!" she said, struggling.

Then, fake Ashley found real Ashley's weapon that we didn't know about, a spear (she got that by pinching a ring that I know Ashley has had for years), and swept me off my feet. Real Lily's dagger went flying somewhere far out of our range.

And some strange force, probably made by Mr. Yin Yang, knocked my sword out of Kayla's hand. It skittered somewhere about three feet away from me.

I thought we were going to lose this battle, when I noticed Kayla. She looked really, really mad.

Her hands caught on fire. Then her arms, then her whole body was in flames.

"This will be the last time you'll ever see light!" she snarled. She gathered up lots of flame in her hands, (though she still was still on fire, completely) and shot them all at the Confuscia.

I thought the floating ball was going to have a heart attack, as well as dying. I mean, he (or she, whatever) was so shocked, then in so much pain. Everybody stopped fighting to watch. Even Ashley, Zoe, and Lily (the real ones) came out of their trance and stared.

"Whoa, she's scary," whimpered Lily.

'Scary' didn't cover it. She was terrifying. Her eyes were blazing red, and she was throwing curses through her gritted teeth. Her whole body was on and surrounded by fire that changed every second from, yellow, to orange, to red, to purple, to blue, to white. Even though flames danced around her, her clothes weren't even scorched.

We couldn't see the Yin Yang anymore, because it was buried in fire. Ash whimpered (or did whatever cats do when they're scared).

Finally Kayla stopped. She collapsed. We rushed to her. She was sprawled on the ground spread eagle, breathing heavily. "That ... was ... awesome," she panted.

"No kidding," said Ashley as we hoisted Kayla up.

"Are we forgetting something?" I wondered out loud. We dared to turn around. Silverstream was still stuck in molten rock, and Moonstruck was half conscious.

"Shoot," said Lily.

My fake friends were getting ready to charge at the sisters. We lunged for them. I managed to grab Black Blade, which was easy to reach, Zoe got out her bow and arrow, Lily found her dagger somewhere, and I told Ashley about her spear/ring.

Real Lily went for fake Lily, real Zoe went for fake Zoe, and real Ashley went for fake Ashley. Kayla and I helped Moonstruck and Silverstream.

(Wow those are long names. How did I not notice that before?) I concentrated, and blasted the rock caked around Silverstream to pieces with my awesome super power of electricity (Superman, whoop, whoop). Then Silverstream and I rushed next to Kayla and Moonstruck.

Moonstruck was almost conscious. We shook her, as the sounds of a small battle roared in our ears. Finally, she woke up.

We told Silverstream to stay with Moonstruck while we rushed to help our friends. But they didn't need our help. The battle was hard—for the enemies. Ashley was having a spear fight. "Curse my duplicate," she uttered as she stabbed fake Ashley, who disintegrated like all the other monsters we defeated. Cocoa chattered with all of the other pets, who were hiding somewhere safe.

Zoe was in a pickle, but then she stopped fighting, as if she was considering a plan. Fake Zoe stopped too, though she seemed to do it because she was wondering what real Zoe was doing. Then real Zoe started to run away. She flashed past me and I

61

thought that she needed help, but she was grinning wildly.

"Running away, you coward?" taunted fake Zoe, although she seemed nervous. Then real Zoe stopped. She turned around, her expression filled with horror. She was looking at something behind fake Zoe, so fake Zoe turned around to see what she was looking at.

Too late. An arrow sprouted from fake Zoe's chest. She only had time to look down, and then she disintegrated.

All of us turned to Lily. She fought like a whirlwind. In fact, she was a whirlwind. Chunks of earth and dirt swirled around her, occasionally flying out and hitting fake Lily's face. Even though fake Lily had knocked real Lily's dagger out of her hand, she fought with her powers. (Ugh, it's so annoying, saying 'real' her and 'fake' her. That battle stunk.) Eventually, she thrust all of the earth at her duplicate.

The duplicate disintegrated just like the other two (duh). We were all worn out. Lily grinned. "Well, that was fun!" she said cheerfully. But I could tell that she was tired.

Moonstruck replied, "Speak for yourself, dirt face. You worked like a storm."

I was confused. "No, I think that was me," I said.

Ashley was confused, too. "Maybe the storm part, but I think I'm a dirt face, too," she said.

Kayla scowled. "Hey, that was pretty cold," she said.

Zoe looked confused. "No, that's me. I'm cold," she countered.

Lily gasped. "You? Cold? Zoe, when you were fighting, electrical flaming sparks flew everywhere," she said. "That sounded better in my head," Lily muttered.

Kayla and I both looked confused. "I think that's us," we said at the same time.

We argued for about five minutes, getting confused with our names and powers and voices, until Silverstream broke us apart. "We should get some rest, all of us," she said.

That night I had trouble sleeping. It was either the fact that this quest was scary and it was going to get scarier, or that creepy Yin Yang. Seriously, that thing will haunt me forever and scare me almost as much as clowns do. Yes, I'm scared of clowns. You got a problem with that?

Anyway, I had trouble sleeping. Thunder the wolf/adorable puppy climbed at my legs and fell asleep on my sleeping bags. Lily's chipmunk, Ashley's chipmunk, Kayla's cat, and Zoe's bunny were all fast asleep at the feet of their owners.

Moonstruck and Silverstream had turned into German Shepherds (they could do that?) and were sleeping on top of their sleeping bags.

I woke up earlier than everybody else. I started to get dressed (behind a tree, of course. It would be so embarrassing if I didn't and one of my friends woke up). After I went out to hunt for food with Thunder.

The forest around Moonstruck's cave was dark and wet. There was an eerie silence. I recalled two years before when I had taken a survival test in woods just like this. Everybody was supposed to go out in the wilderness, and whoever stayed in the forest longest would receive a prize. The judges would stay in a nice, warm, cabin just outside of the woods (to make it more tempting to come out. It was pretty harsh). If you got too scared or hurt or you couldn't take it anymore, you could go to the cabin and they would give you a room, but that meant that you failed the test. After three weeks, the judges would come and get you. They gave you nothing except for clothes during the test. It was a long time.

The first day of the survival test, I figured out how to walk silently. (I actually scared a boy that I hated.) I figured that I would need some shelter, so I gathered lots of large sticks and branches, and then I found a large tree that separated into two trunks. I found some grass and tied it together to make a large rope, then tied one end to all of my sticks. Then I put the other end in my mouth and started climbing the tree.

When I got to the top, I tied it to a strong branch. Then I climbed down, found a very heavy rock, and brought it up the tree again. Then I untied the rope, tied the rock to it, and put it on the other side of the branch. The rock went down, the sticks came up. The rock was heavier than the sticks. Do the math and stop interrupting my flashback.

I laid the sticks above where the trunk split. The perfect shelter. If you're in a wilderness contest, of course. I figured that I would need some food for the next three weeks. The Internet had said it would snow the next day.

I built up my strength. I didn't know how I was so good at surviving, but my instinct told me. I found a triangular rock and a circular one. Then I found another large stick. I made some more rope and tied the triangle rock to the stick that made a blunt spear. I sharpened it with the circle rock.

Finally, I had a good spear. But how would I find my way back? I figured it out (double duh). I found some soft bark, and wrapped it to make the form of a cone. Then I filled the inside with three small pinecones. Then I stuck it in the ground. No, I'm not done yet.

There was a stream nearby. I cupped some water in my hands, and spread it around the area with the bark that I stuck in the ground. I kept doing that until the ground around the cone was completely wet.

Then I found some flint (no idea why it was there). A lot of flint, actually. I gathered up all of the flint that I could carry, and brought it up to my shelter. I made a small but strong basket out of thick weeds and put all the flint inside of it. Then I brought two pieces down to the cone and rubbed and mashed them together. One of them caught fire. I dropped that one into the cone, in which the pinecones caught on fire. Voila. A torch made by an eight year old, that would be bright enough to lead my way back.

I took my spear and went into the deep woods. Finally, I heard a crackling sound. I used my technique for walking silently and crept up to the sound, my spear ready. The sound stopped. It was a big deer. Perfect. I aimed my spear and got it square on the side.

The deer fell. I ran to it, looking around for anybody else in the contest, almost daring my luck. Nobody was around. I tied some spare string around the deer and hauled it to and up my 'tree house.' I skinned the meat. Then I made another basket out of weeds and put the meat in it. Suddenly I remembered that I wasn't the only one in this test.

As if on cue, a boy came swinging through the trees on a rope similar to the one I made. "Aaaaaaiiiiiiiaaaaa!!!" he yelled as he swung towards my shelter. He might steal my food! I was quick to think. I grabbed my spear. I almost glanced behind me at the stream, but there was no time for that. I stood up, my spear ready.

When the boy was right over my shelter and about to drop down, I swung my spear and cut his rope. The boy plunged into the river. I set my spear down.

The river. I needed water. So I cut some sturdy weeds into little long pieces. Then I wove them together in a filter. I climbed down by the river and felt around it.

I hit a soft spot. *Clay*. I dug up as much as I could. Finally, I got enough. I formed a pot. It dried pretty quickly, but while it was doing that I picked the pines off of an evergreen tree to eat along with the meat. When I was done, I put them all in another basket that I made. Then I got the water.

By then the pot was dry. It wasn't the prettiest, but it was solid. I put it close to the stream along with the filter. Then I scooped up water with the filter and quickly held it over the pot, just in time for the water to cleanse and go into the pot. Finally, I had enough water for one week.

I climbed up the tree with my water and pines. Then I used the torch that I made to roast the meat and used the deerskin for blankets.

I kept doing that every week, and once I even got sick. But I scraped the bark off a willow tree and cured that. (Seriously, this forest has everything.)

I snapped into the present. I was alone in the woods near Moonstruck's cave at four in the morning, hunting for food. (Listen to that flashback, kids. It will help if you need to survive in the woods.)

I walked silently along the forest floor, my sword ready. Then I heard a stick snap, and I rushed to the sound, still not making any noise. There was a big stag eating grass. I lifted my sword.

The stag fell to the ground. Then I walked up to it, poked it, and then I felt satisfied. I skinned the stag and left the skin behind, so Ashley and Zoe wouldn't freak.

I dragged the meat all the way back to Moonstruck's cave and set it down near my sleeping bag. Then I picked some evergreen pines (just like in my flashback) and set those next to the meat.

I shook Kayla awake softly. She groaned, and woke up to see me standing over a pile o' meat, smiling. She woke up completely. Then she walked over to me.

"What's with the meat and waking me up?" she asked.

I smiled. "I want breakfast to be ready when they wake up," I said.

70

"You call this breakfast?" Kayla scoffed. I nodded. She sighed, as if to say, *I had to be the fire person.*

I brought in some sticks (don't ask where I found them) and Kayla set them ablaze. Then I used a weed rope and hung the meat over the fire, twisting it every so often. Then I sprinkled the evergreen pines on it to add more flavor.

Kayla and I sat down while we were waiting for the meat to cook. Then Silverstream woke up and joined the conversation.

"So, I've been wanting to ask…" Kayla said nervously. Then she suddenly sat up straight and looked into Silverstream's eyes with a big smile on her face. Her big, brown eyes were hard to resist. "What are all the other Magic types?" she asked eagerly.

Silverstream was surprised by the sudden happiness. "Well, let me see, there's the ones you know—storm, fire, earth, ice, and universe. Then there's ones that you don't know—precious metals, mechanics, water, and the most dangerous—myth."

71

Silverstream said *myth* so darkly that I could tell that it was a hard and uncommon Magic type. We were silent for a few seconds.

Suddenly, Kayla said happily, "Food's ready!" We went over to check. It was a big, slightly red, meat.

Silverstream was shocked. "You guys made this?" she exclaimed. We nodded. "It looks and smells amazing!" she said. We inhaled the scent of the meat.

"Well, let's wake up the others!" said Kayla.

Kayla shook Zoe gently. I whispered to Ashley and Lily. They all woke up. We looked over at Silverstream. She was shaking Moonstruck as hard as she could.

"Can you guys help? She won't wake up!" Silverstream huffed. Zoe stepped forward, but I held her back then I stepped forward. I held my hand to the sky. Clouds formed outside the cave and suddenly, BOOM!!!

Everybody had closed their eyes. Smart friends. When we opened them we saw a smoking and wide-eyed Moonstruck who was definitely awake. We all fell to the floor laughing. Even Silverstream. It was hilarious to see someone so powerful surprised by being electrocuted by a ten-year-old.

"Why I'm gonna…" said Moonstruck, then she sniffed the air. "Is that, breakfast?" she asked. "'Cause that smells dee-licious!"

Kayla and I were surprised. "You like it?" we asked at the same time.

"You two made this? When do we get to eat?" she asked eagerly.

"Now," I laughed.

Everybody wolfed the food down except for Kayla and me. We wanted to make it last. Snowy, Thunder, Puffy, Cocoa, and Ash all ran around us, hoping for a scrap or something. I gave Thunder a reasonable piece of my meat. He liked it.

"So I have a theory," I said. All eyes turned to me. "Remember what I said about all of our crowns?" Zoe's hand drifted towards her backpack. "Well, think about it. We've been picking up jewels the whole way around this galaxy." Ashley seemed to

73

consider the idea. "Maybe, we are supposed to find a jewel from each planet of each element, except for universe, and put them all together, to make the jewel we're looking for!"

Moonstruck nodded. "But why not universe?" she asked.

I smiled. "Because, the universe jewel is the one we'll get if we put the other ones together."

Moonstruck smiled. Lily looked confused. "But what about storm? We passed that place a while ago and we found no jewel," she said.

I tossed her a dark blue opal. She just barely caught it. "I found this on our way out. Happy now?" I asked. She nodded.

Zoe scratched her head. "But that's too easy. Are you sure it's not some… random jewel?"

I glared at her. "Fine, I'll show you. I found out that I could do it this morning," I sighed. (By the way, I did not explain this to you folks when I went hunting.)

I clutched the rock in my hands and held it above my head. I stood up and closed my eyes, still holding up the opal. For a few seconds nothing happened.

Lily laughed weakly. "Did you really think that…" her voice faltered.

Then wind swirled around me. Dust and vapor rolled in. I glowed black. Was that even possible? (I think I said that before.) Then I put the rock down.

The wind stopped. The dust moved where it was before, and the black glow faded. My friends just stared in amazement.

Finally, Ashley broke the tension. "So… where to next?" she asked.

We started to pack up. It was hard to stuff my sleeping bag into my puny backpack. There was a huge weight on my shoulders. It was probably that I was worried. I think that my friends were scared of what I did. I was scared of what I did. Everybody was silent as we trudged out of Moonstruck's cave.

I felt really guilty. Like I said, they were probably scared of what I did, and they would be nervous to talk to me. That lump of guilt stayed as we followed Silverstream to the next planet.

"Uggghhhh!!!" Lily complained. The planet we were going to next was so far away! My feet ached.

"Where are we going?" asked Kayla.

Silverstream looked tired of answering this question, even though it was the first time we asked.

"We are…." Suddenly Silverstream stopped.

We ran into her, which was unpleasant for Moonstruck, who was in the middle.

"There it is!" Silverstream said proudly. I looked in the direction she was pointing.

There was a planet, but it wasn't solid. It was blue and the surface was churning. There were little dots swarming around it. It was a very pretty sight, with the stars and black around it. I so wished I had a camera that could take pictures from the magic realm.

I realized that Silverstream was walking towards the planet. I ran up to her and grabbed her shoulder.

"Whoa, you can't just walk up to that planet. It isn't solid. It might be dange…" I said firmly, but my voice faltered.

Silverstream looked at me. Her eyes were pure gold and her expression was deadly calm. I quickly let go, surprised. Moonstruck walked up at a normal pace (which is abnormal for her), her face also calm and her eyes gold.

I looked back at my friends for help. They shrugged but Lily stepped forward. "They got possessed by a protection spell," she said. "The spell is supposed to keep universe types out."

I was surprised. "How did you know that?" I asked.

"A little sign said that as he walked by," she said.

I raised an eyebrow. "I'm sorry?"

As if on cue, a little sign that read *Careful - Protection Spell to Keep out Universe Types* walked past us.

"Right... I will label this planet's gravity circle as *weird*. Walking signs, confirmed." I said.

"Uh, remember our good friends the dragons who are currently possessed by a planet that we don't know about but they do?" asked Lily.

I glared at her. "You know just what to say don't you!" I snapped. She shrugged.

I sighed. "Okay, let's follow our friendly friends the dragons on to this stupid planet," I grumbled.

CHAPTER FOUR THE WATER PLANET

Getting attacked by flesh-eating eels was not my idea (just saying). They had long, sleek black bodies four times the size of a regular eel. They had three eyes, all glowing red, none of which had pupils, which was creepy. Their mouths were perfect ovals filled with two rows of razor teeth. Their backs had one long very sharp looking spike.

We couldn't stop Moonstruck and Silverstream from walking towards the planet, partly because when Ashley tried to do it Moonstruck blasted her backward, so we had no choice but to follow them.

The planet was farther away than I thought. It seemed that the closer we got, if I didn't keep my eyes on it, it would move farther away.

Correct me. I was so distracted that I ran into some eels. I was embarrassed so I looked up at the eel to say something, but no words came out. He looked just like I said (explanation in the front of this chapter—flesh-eating eel), but this was the first one we saw. Apparently, he was surprised to see me, too.

We started to have a conversation that went like this...

The eel hissed.

"Hiss... whatever that means," I said.

He seemed satisfied with that. "Na no wri?" he demanded.

I staggered backward. *These things could talk as well?*

"Um… eh, wri na no," I said. I was just guessing, but I knew immediately that I had said the wrong thing. He darted at me.

At least I had *some* practice. My instinct screamed *duck!* But I knew better. I opened Black Blade and instinctively deflected his attack. But he was still faster (dang, I feel so slow under water). His teeth clinked against my sword, and the razor on his back started sword fighting with me.

I dared to glance back. Zoe and Ashley were looking at me with worry, and Lily and Kayla were wrestling Silverstream and Moonstruck down, trying to get them to snap out of it.

From somewhere behind me Ashley yelled, "Hey! Let me fight him. After all, I do have a spear that easily matches his spike." I thought out of the corner of my eye I saw her smirk on that last sentence.

I nodded. I looked up at the eel and smiled a dumb smile. "See you later, fang face. And, don't look behind you," I said.

81

He turned slowly. But it was too late. The last thing he saw was Ashley's spear coming down on his face. Smart girl. She had snuck up behind fish face and pounced. Thunder yapped in approval. His image flickered from a happy dog to a happy wolf, and then back to a dog.

I smiled. "That was awesome," I said.

Ashley sighed. "Let's hope no one saw that," she said. "We want to make friends with this place."

We walked toward the blue planet when I ran into another something. Wait no, I'm sorry. I fell into something. All I could see was moving blue, my clothes were wet, and I couldn't breathe. *Stupid me.* I thought. *This is the water planet. How did I not see that?*

I managed to open my eyes. There was water all around me and there was something that seemed to be the spirits of the eels ('cause as far as I'm concerned, I didn't see anything else). Talk about creepy.

I was starting to turn blue. Any second now I wouldn't be able to hold my breath…

Two people hoisted me up. I sprawled at their feet, coughing and sputtering.

"Oh derp! Oh derp, oh derp, oh derp! You were down there for so long! Oh derp!"

I tried to visualize who had said that. It was Lily's voice. I'd never in my life heard it so full of worry.

Zoe draped a towel over me. It was just then that I realized how cold and drenched I was. I shivered when Zoe touched me. (I wasn't sure if it was Zoe's ice powers or the fact that I was soaked.)

"Look!" said Zoe suddenly. I looked. Funny how that works with humans, when someone tells you not to look, they look. (This is the opposite and not the point.)

Silverstream and Moonstruck were still walking to the planet of water. "Eesh," I muttered. "They can't go there. Stupid dragons." We ran to them, with Zoe in the lead.

Suddenly, Zoe stopped. "Look again," she said. We looked. Again. A tunnel was opening where

Silverstream and Moonstruck were. They walked inside.

"We should follow them," said Kayla.

Agreed. We ran in just as the tunnel was starting to close.

The tunnel was dark. We could breathe, so I guessed this was meant for non-water types. The door shut behind us.

Forget dark. I couldn't see my hand in front of my face. I felt around for my friends. Then I bumped into something that I hoped was one of them. "Ow," groaned the voice of Lily. I exhaled.

Suddenly a light turned on. *There are lights in here?* I thought. Nope. Ashley screamed. I turned and saw her face to face with a fish. Don't think that is stupid. The fish had giant sharp teeth, huge glassy eyes, and a little light bulb hanging from its head. *Anglerfish,* I thought.

I looked back at Ashley. She was still freaked out, but she gently pushed the fish away. The fish blew a bubble. "What?" Ashley asked the fish.

"Yay!" said Lily.

"Huh?" I said.

"Um, what did he say?" asked Zoe. (Remember this: Lily and Ashley are earth types. They can talk to animals and fish and stuff. If you already knew that, good for you. I was talking to the people who forgot.)

"He said that he would lead us to Silverstream and Moonstruck," translated Ashley.

"You are going to trust that thing?" asked Zoe. The anglerfish lowered his head.

Lily held her head high. "Well, I trust him. Besides, we're trapped. If you want to shoo him off, then where would we go? He has given us an offer, and we should take it. I don't want to let him down," she said. Zoe was silent.

We followed the fish not very far when I heard a little yap. I turned around.

"Aw, man! We left our little buddies behind. Uh, mister fish? Can you get them out?" asked Zoe.

Thunder whimpered. Ash scratched the sea wall. Snowy tried to jump through it and banged her head. Puffy tried to use Cocoa as a battering ram.

85

I ran to the wall. The anglerfish followed. Ashley frowned. "We have to leave them behind. Sorry, *he* said that. Can you tell them that we'll be right back?" she asked the fish. The anglerfish blew a bubble and the pets sat down.

"This fish is so cool," Lily muttered. We followed him down the dark tunnel, our way lit by the little lamp thingy on his head.

Eventually, we stopped. The fish glowed at a gate. "Wait, you're not coming?" asked Ashley. The anglerfish nodded his head sadly.

I sighed. "Okay," I said. "Let's find our friends and get out of here."

We walked through the gate. "Whoa," said Lily. "Eel-otropolis." I looked where she was looking.

There was New York underwater on a different planet—coral buildings, fish and eels swimming busily all around paths of sand. I could see coral apartments, some with eels watering kelp and seaweed on their porches. (Is that even possible underwater?)

It kind of made me homesick for New York. I promised myself that I would go back to my favorite pancake restaurant, sometime, whether this stupid quest was done or not.

We walked through the streets casually, hoping no one would notice us. They didn't. It *was* just like New York. They wouldn't care if a giant hamster came rolling through the streets in a hamster ball covered with multi-colored polka dots.

We kept walking until we got to a long pathway that was lined by eel guards. At the end was a giant coral castle. (Is everything made out of coral? There's one more thing than New York has.)

We walked down the aisle. Surprisingly, none of the eel guards tried to stop us. As we walked, bubbles fizzled from beneath our feet. Awkward!

We stood in front of it. "Mama mia," muttered Lily as we gazed up the castle. It was much prettier up close. By the way, that pathway was like a quarter mile long, with guards down the whole thing. They must really need to protect this chunk of coral a.k.a. castle.

"So, how do we get in? I mean, assuming that Moonstruck and Silverstream are in there," I said.

Lily rolled her eyes. "Maybe we press the button right here that says *drawbridge*."

I felt my face get hot. While I glared at Lily, who was currently smirking like she does when she's right, Zoe pressed the button, and a giant coral—like I said, *everything* is coral—drawbridge came down and landed at our feet. It would've squashed Kayla flat if she was a foot closer.

"Eeep," said wide-eyed Kayla. We stared at her for like thirty seconds (this time I have no idea why), and then shook it off. We started across the bridge.

(Thought moment below)

You know, I really had no idea why they had a bridge. I mean, there wasn't a moat or anything. Actually, since this whole planet was made of water, they couldn't even make a moat. So the only reason that they would use the drawbridge would be a change of scenery so the eels that patroled the quarter mile aisle wouldn't get bored. I wouldn't blame them.

(Thought moment over)

I stared at the entry with my sword ready, as if waiting for a monster or eel to jump out and attack or something.

"Uh, good job doing the staring contest with the castle, but are we going to go in now?" asked Lily. Her voice made me jump. I nodded and entered the castle.

The room was big and blue (naturally). There was a staircase in front of us. A big chandelier hung above us with dozens of little aquamarines. The marble floor made a squeaking sound if I slid. We entered the middle of the room.

I'd never had much feeling for Thunder, which was kinda mean, but this was the first time ever that I really missed that guy. I wish I had that cute little puppy by my side who could turn into a giant fierce (but on our side) wolf any time an attacker would come. I sighed.

Suddenly I heard footsteps. Everybody took out their weapons. Kayla took out a big rock that she found somewhere. Zoe accidently shot like four arrows.

We heard, THUNK, THUNK, THUNK, THUNK! I squeezed my eyes shut. When I opened them, I saw a girl our age. She had long blond hair and aquamarine eyes. She was wearing a long blue dress (was everything here blue?), and she was hiding her face in her arms and holding up one leg. Behind her, stuck to the wall, were Zoe's four arrows.

"Goodness me!" the girl said, stepping away from the wall.

Zoe bit her lip. "Oopsy! Gosh, I'm so sorry!" she stammered, running towards the girl and plucking her arrows out of the wall.

"It's okay," the girl said, brushing the dust off her dress.

"Um, weird way to meet someone," I said. "What's your name?"

The girl pulled down her sleeve. "Lucy," she said.

Ashley hung her head. "Oooh!" she groaned. "I've always wanted that name!"

Lucy looked at her. It was harder to see earlier, but now I could see her facial details more. Lucy had blue eyes just like Zoe's, but Lucy's were darker. Her eyes were wise and sad, like she remembered something.

"I have always wanted that name, *Ashley*," Lucy said dreamily.

Ashley looked shocked. "How the heck did you know my name?" she asked.

"A little chipmunk told me. He was waiting at the barrier," Lucy answered.

A little chipmunk peered out from her legs. "Cocoa!" Ashley cried. Cocoa ran to her. "How did he get in?"

Lucy smiled smugly. "Like I said, he was waiting at the barrier with another one of his kind. I let him in."

Lily looked at her hopefully. "You have Puffy?" she asked.

"Who is Puffy…?"

Another little chipmunk came from behind Lucy's dress. Puffy leaped into Lily's arms. "Smart, fluffy, chipmunk!" said Ashley.

Lucy raised her eyebrow. "These are yours, I suppose?" Ashley and Lily nodded vigorously.

Zoe turned to Lucy. "Um, by any chance, was anybody else there?"

Lucy stroked her chin. "No," she said. "I didn't see anybody except for these two."

I was shocked. "Wait, nobody? But what about Thunder?" I asked.

"And Snowy?" said Zoe.

"And Ash?" added Kayla.

"There were others?" asked Lucy. We nodded. "Well…"

Ashley stopped her to listen to what Cocoa had to say. "Eel guards took them away," she said.

"What!" said Kayla.

"Eel guards?" asked Lucy. "What are those?"

"Oh," I said. "Eel guards are really creepy giant eels with three eyes and no pupils, so you can't tell where they're looking. They are guarding like, everywhere."

Lucy thought for a moment, and then she laughed. "Oh! You mean the Oduoccë."

"What?" I asked.

(Thought moment below)

Oduoccë is pronounced like OH-DEW-AWCH-EE.

(Thought moment over)

"Is that some Italian word?" asked Lily. "No, its Maga," replied Lucy. "You should know. You're Magics, right?" We nodded. "Then you should know Maga. It's our language. I am a Magic, too."

"Cool!" said Ashley.

"Anyway, about your furry friends, I know something about them," Lucy said. "I was in my room, when one of the Oduoccë came up and told me that they got new prisoners. I was on my way to see who they were, when THUNKETY THUNK, THUNK, THUNK! I almost got hit by four out of control arrows."

Zoe shuffled her feet.

"Luckily, they were out of control, like I said, so they missed." Lucy made an imitation of what happened with her hands. Then she spread her arms and looked directly at us. "Then I met you guys!"

She stood there smiling and we stood there blinking. I cleared my throat. "Um, nice... explanation," I said.

Lucy nodded in agreement. "So, come to my room with me," she said. "Let's talk about our...ah, situation," she said.

Again, Lucy's room was all blue. The bedspread was blue, her desk was blue, closet, carpet, bed itself, lights, walls, ceiling, and chair were all blue.

"So, you live here? This is your planet? You're a queen?" asked Zoe.

"Princess," Lucy admitted. "And yes, I live here. And this is my planet. After all, I cannot leave..." her voice drifted as she gazed out her bedroom window.

"Anyway," she said, her voice becoming firmer and her expression becoming sadder. "What brought you here?"

I explained what we did. Our quest, going to the water element planet, Silverstream and Moonstruck getting under a spell, all up until we met Lucy.

"Oh, a quest. So cool. I used to be cool." Lucy muttered every now and then. Her eyes glanced out the window, and then back at me. I wondered if something had happened...

"So, basically, you're on a quest to find the crown jewel, and every jewel that you pick from each planet is one piece of the original gem, and you have all of the jewels of your elements, so now you're trying to find the jewels of other elements, and you ended up here first, so you tried to come, but when you crossed the barrier your friends got cast under that spell, so you tried to help by getting them back, but Rachel here accidently stepped into the wrong side of the planet and almost drowned, but you pulled her up, and then realized that your friends were walking to my visitor tunnel, so you followed them, but they were too far away and it was pitch black, so you were guided by my friend the anglerfish, and he left you at the gates, so you walked

95

through my city until you got to my extremely long walkway, which it was not my choice to make it so long, until you entered my castle, and heard my footsteps, and you took out your weapons and almost killed me." Lucy spoke so fast it made my head spin.

I tried to speak, but no words came out. We stared at her. "Well?" she asked. "Is that correct?"

We nodded. "So, um, can you take us to our friends?" I asked.

Lucy led us down dark corridors (made of blue marble, of course) until we got to a dark hallway lit only by a few light bulbs. On the sides of the hallway were smaller cells with bars across the front, wrapped in seaweed. Funny. All of the cells were empty.

"I have the key," said Lucy. "The guards will only let them out if I approve."

"Please approve," pleaded Lily.

We followed her to Moonstruck and Silverstream's cell. On the way, we passed one that was captive. There was something white, orange, and black and gray. "Hold on a second. Let's go back to that cell," I said, pointing to the one I saw.

We backed up. In the cell I was pointing to were the little cute animals that we had adopted on this quest. "Yay!" said Lily, clapping her hands together and jumping up and down.

Lucy looked at us. "These are your pets?"

We nodded. "I wouldn't really call them 'pets', but yes. They are. Could you let them out?" Ashley asked. Lucy nodded and smiled.

"Yay!" Lily said again, doing the same motion that she did the first time.

When Thunder saw me, he sprang up, ran to the bars, yapping and wagging his tail so hard that he turned into a wolf again. Lucy stepped back. "Whoa," she said. "Is that normal?"

Kayla laughed. "Of course! Well, if you put it one way, nothing is normal here, but yes. He does that when someone attacks, or when he's really excited." Kayla glanced at Thunder, who was currently chasing his tail, poofing from puppy to wolf on every turn. "And he's really excited," she said again.

We watched as Lucy grabbed a key off its hook and turned it in the lock. Thunder ran to me and so did the other 'pets'. Lucy smiled. "Now for your friends," she said.

We were led to a big cage. The cage had two sleeping tigers in it. "Err, are you sure that these are your friends? They look more like … felines," said Lucy.

Lily rolled her eyes. "Universe types are shape-shifters. Let me show you," she said.

Lily stepped forward and took a deep breath. "THERE'S A BATTLE GOING ON!" she shouted.

There was a poof, and Moonstruck sat up with a jolt, wide eyed. She was back in human form. "Who, what, where am I?" she asked.

Lucy unlocked the cage that she was in. "Hi. You must be the friends that these guys have been talking about," she said.

Once Moonstruck and Silverstream got out of the cage, and Lucy invited them to her room, they asked Lucy some questions.

"So you're a water type," Silverstream said. Lucy nodded. "This is your planet? You live here? The Oduoccë serve you?"

Lucy nodded after all of them. "Yes," she said. "This is my planet. I live here. The Oduoccë serve me. Not the most pleasant beings, but they're fine…." Her voice drifted again. She looked longingly out the window.

Silverstream looked at her with concern, but Lucy averted her gaze. Silverstream looked at Moonstruck, who was scowling—she's very good at that—at Lily. Silverstream sighed, as if confirming that she wouldn't be any help.

"Lucy," said Silverstream. "May I have your hand?" Lucy put her hand in Silverstream's without hesitation.

Silverstream closed her eyes, running her fingers across Lucy's palm. Zoe backed up. Suddenly, Silverstream opened her eyes. But they weren't the same stormy gray. They were the exact same eyes as Lucy's, aquamarine.

Lucy sat around calmly, her hand still in Silverstream's, as if nothing was happening. Silverstream spoke in Lucy's voice. "I have been trapped here," she said. All attention turned toward Silverstream. "I was on a quest, and I decided to visit my planet. They made me their princess, and they gave me everything except for the ability to go home. I could never leave this place."

I thought that this must be Lucy's past.

"The only way I could've gotten away would be to be chaperoned by a universe type. That is why the Oduoccë put a spell on the gravity circle." Silverstream spoke Lucy's voice, but Lucy was still looking out the window. (Man, Silverstream is über nice, but sometimes she's just creepy. Not the point.) I noticed that Lucy's mouth was moving, not Silverstream's. But Lucy's voice was still coming out Silverstream's mouth.

(Thought moment below)

Two words. Creepy and confusing. ("and" is not included as one of the two words. Neither is this.)

(Thought moment over)

Silverstream's eyes cleared to their normal color.

Lucy looked back at us and smiled. "Would you like me to help you pack for your quest?" she asked.

I talked with everybody while Lucy packed for us (which was REALLY nice of her). "I think she should come with us," I said. Everybody nodded in agreement except for Moonstruck, who was still staring at Lily (though she took a break from that just to stare at her sister do the creepy mind-reading thing).

"Ready!" called Lucy happily. She was holding three big duffel bags, with four more at her feet.

"Wow," said Zoe. "We didn't even have time to help." Lily, Ashley, Kayla, Moonstruck, and Silverstream all laughed. Suddenly I remembered why we came here in the first place.

"Lucy," I said. "Do you happen to have the water element jewel?"

Lucy's smile got even brighter. "Of course I do! Hold on a sec," she said, as she ran up the giant stairway.

She stopped at the top and faced her aquamarine chandelier. Her eyes fixed on a small one in the middle. Then she ran to a closet and got out the longest pole ever. She put one end on the ground at the bottom of the staircase. Then her eyes directed toward the little aquamarine again.

It was too late when I realized what she was going to do. She held the other end of the pole firmly. Then she pushed forward and her feet went off the ground.

I watched as she soared through the air, riding on the pole. Right when she passed the chandelier, she grabbed the little jewel and came down to meet the ground.

There was no time to run and catch her, but that was not needed. She landed softly on a mattress. (Where did that come from?) Then she walked over and handed me the jewel. I held it in my hands, staring.

Lily bowed like a-million times saying, "I will follow in your footsteps. Forever!"

I slipped the jewel in my pocket. "Lucy, I've been wanting to ask," I said. "Would you like to come on the quest with us?"

Lucy dropped the bags that she was holding. "I- I couldn't," she stammered.

I rolled my eyes. "Yes, you could. Now let's sneak out of here."

CHAPTER FIVE ESCAPE EXCEPT FOR ONE

Sneaking out was easy. Getting past the Oduoccë was not. Lucy had handed each of us a bag, and we stuffed our pets into them. Lucy had promised that there were small holes in the bags so they wouldn't suffocate. Thunder would not have liked that.

Lucy had led us through the back door, which led to a little path that went straight to the visitor tunnel door.

The pathway was a lot like the route to this planet. You got closer by every step, but when you looked away or even blinked, the door would seem far away.

After what seemed like a mile (drum roll…) it was still farther away. I think that the Oduoccë did that, so any universe type who tried to save Lucy would get really tired getting here. But universe types can power up whenever they want. Huh.

I was about to look back at my friends to see what they were doing when CLONK! I hit my head on something hard. "Ow," I groaned.

Lily stepped forward. "Great! You found the door even though it wasn't where you thought it would be," she said.

She felt around for it where I had hit. But it wasn't where she thought it would be either. Then I thought I saw something shimmer ahead of us.

"What…." Lucy grabbed Lily and me by the hand and started to run forward, gesturing for the others to follow. "Quick! We don't want to lose it!"

Lucy dragged us faster and faster every time that we saw the shimmer. Sometimes I could see the full image. It was a shiny dark brown with ivy vines curling around it. But every time I saw a part of the image, the door vanished and reappeared farther away from us. Every time that happened, Lucy would run faster.

We saw another shimmer, and a flash image of the door. Moonstruck lunged for it and landed hard on the ground. Lucy ran faster.

Another image flashed. Zoe and Kayla leapt for it and face-planted on a small flower patch. Lucy ran faster. Lily struggled out of Lucy's grip and ran ahead, even though we didn't see the door yet. But she kept running ahead of us.

Lucy tried to stay only a little behind, but Lily was fast. Still, Lucy managed to keep up. Once said, and once more, not the point.

Suddenly the door appeared next to Lily. She noticed it, and when it was about to disappear, she lunged and grabbed the handle. The door stayed in place.

We stood there, huffing and puffing for a minute, with Lily still holding the door in its place. "Wow," I said in between breaths. "I knew you were funny, but I didn't know you were smart, too."

Lily rolled her eyes. (We do that a lot, just a heads up.) "Ha ha. I got the door. Now get in before I lose my grip."

Moonstruck started to the door. She was just about to reach for the doorknob, when a spear struck the door, just missing her.

"What the..." I started to say. Even if I had finished, Moonstruck wouldn't have noticed me. She was too busy staring at the spear that had almost skewered her face.

She shook out of it. I glanced behind me. I don't know if it was the right or wrong thing to do. There was an army of Oduoccë marching to us. I thought that they thought (ugh) that we were taking their princess. Thunder and the other animals hopped out of our bags. Ash set on fire, Cocoa and Puffy had a rope ready, Snowy made a snow wall above the Oduoccë, and Thunder changed to his wolf form.

"Okay, that wolf form is super cool," Lucy admitted.

The animals looked at her hopefully. "Go ahead!" she laughed.

Ash ran forward, setting some of the Oduoccë on fire. Cocoa and Puffy ran around the eels, tying them up. Snowy let the snow wall come crashing down on all of them, and after they were dazed, Thunder pounced on them and started attacking.

"Dude," said Lily. "Best. Animals. Ever." We agreed.

I patted my pocket to make sure that the jewel was still there. It was. I looked back up at the battle. It was going well, but the pets were slowing down. Cocoa and Puffy retreated because they were out of rope. Thunder's image flickered every time he dodged an attack.

I started forward to help, but Lucy signaled *stop*. "I will hold them back. You go through the door," she said.

"What? No! You can't! You can't escape without a universe chaperone!" said Zoe.

Lucy took a deep breath. "I know. Your prophecy said '*Since this is your second quest.*' It would be my first. I don't think I was meant to be on this one," she said.

I protested, but she told Moonstruck and Silverstream to lead us to the next planet. I could tell that they didn't want to leave her either, but they opened the door and pushed us through.

The last image I saw of the water planet was Lucy drowning in Oduoccë. I felt for the jewel in my pocket. Still there.

"Wait," said Ashley suddenly. "If we're on the water planet, then how are we breathing?"

CHAPTER SIX MECHANICS

Two people hoisted me up. I sprawled at their feet, coughing and sputtering.

"Oh derp! Oh derp, oh derp, oh derp! You were down there for so long! Oh derp!"

I tried to visualize who had said that. It was Lily's voice. I'd never in my life heard it so full of worry.

Zoe draped a towel over me. It was just then that I realized how cold and drenched I was. I shivered when Zoe touched me. (I wasn't sure if it was Zoe's ice powers or the fact that I was soaked.)

Was the water planet just a dream? I patted my pocket. The jewel was there. Weird things can happen when you're in the magic universe. Silverstream and Moonstruck hunched over me.

"Your spell got broken?" I asked.

Moonstruck looked at me funny. "What spell?" she asked.

"Never mind. And the pets?" I asked.

"Right here," said Kayla.

"Right," I said. "Let's get to the next planet."

Ashley looked confused. "But what about this planet?" she asked.

I touched my pocket again. "All good. Let's go," I said smiling. I guess they will never know what happened at the water planet.

As we walked, I showed them the jewel. "Wow," said Kayla. "Did it like, magically appear in your pocket?" Then she turned red. "Sheesh. I'm so stupid. Magically. I'm walking on air, with magical fire powers, with two dragons…"

111

"Hey!" complained Moonstruck.

Kayla went on, "... and I think that a rock appearing in your pocket is magical? Wow. I'm so off."

Ashley turned to Silverstream. "Where to next?" she asked.

"Precious metals," Silverstream said.

Moonstruck rubbed her hands together.

"No," said Silverstream firmly without even looking at her.

"Aw, come on," complained Moonstruck.

Silverstream rocked back and forth on her heels. "The great and powerful Moonstruck, complaining that she can't steal some jewels," she said. Moonstruck growled and lunged for her, but Silverstream simply moved out of the way. Moonstruck landed hard.

"Let's be on our way," said Silverstream. She was totally poker faced, but I could see that she was hiding a smile.

After a while, I saw the planet. But I was hungry. "Let's sit down and have some food," I said.

Nobody argued. When we were done, we started to the planet again.

Five minutes later, I got a better view. It looked like a giant, sparkling jewel. No, four jewels.

Wrong again. It looked it was made of thousands of different kinds of jewels. We were walking to an inside-out jewel mine.

I don't know what reminded me, but I asked, "Silverstream? How did I know that this guy named Locious had to hold up the sky, not us?"

Silverstream smiled. "I told you. I made it enter your head," she answered. "But that's not important. We're here."

I looked ahead. The planet with thousands of jewels stood just in front of us. We stepped onto it. Soft gemstones crunched under my feet.

Soon we came up to a boy who was throwing gems at a target and watching them crumble. "Hey, you can't do that! You're wasting them!" said Zoe suddenly.

The boy frowned and looked at us. "Hey, what's with the big group of girls? Not even a boy can find his way here," he said. "And I'm not wasting them. Look."

We watched as the boy picked up a ruby and threw it straight at the target. It hit right in the middle and shattered to the ground. Thunder yapped and surprised him.

"See? It's just…" Zoe started.

But the boy held up his hand and Zoe stopped. A few seconds later, four rubies popped up where the other one had shattered. Zoe put on an admiring smile.

The boy held out his hand. "My name is Austin," he said. "Wanna' see me do more throwing?"

"We would love to, but we're looking for something," I said.

Austin stroked his chin. "What might that be?" he asked.

"Your element jewel," I replied.

"Jewel?" Austin asked. "Well, that's going to be hard to find." He turned to face mountains of jewels.

"How about this," he said. "I will help you, if you do me a favor."

"Deal," I said.

"Then all aboard the Austin train!"

The Austin train was slow. If I had a giant slug, he and the slug would be twins. A few times, he tripped over Cocoa and Puffy until Ashley and Lily told them to stop.

"Hey, what's that on your wrist?" Ashley asked.

Austin looked at it. "Oh, it's just a watch. Why do you ask?"

Ashley frowned. "There's something on it," she said.

"Like this jewel?" he asked.

"Yes. Could you hand it to me?" she asked.

Austin plucked the jewel off of his watch and handed it to Ashley. She examined it.

"Hold this above your head and concentrate," she said, handing the gem back.

Austin looked at her funny. "Okay. You guys are weird, but okay," he said.

He held it above his head. I guessed that he was concentrating, because the wind started to swirl around him and the jewel. Gems around him went up in the air and started glowing. He put the jewel down and the wind stopped. The gems went back to their place.

"You know," said Ashley. "I think that's your element—jewel." Austin rolled his eyes.

"Oh, gee. You think?"

Thunder yapped and changed to a wolf. Austin screamed. "Look!" he said, pointing to him.

I ruffled Thunder's fur. "Ya. This is my dog," I said. Then I put my finger on my lower lip. "Oh wait. I guess I can't have an awesome dog because I'm a *girl*. Well, nobody told me." My friends giggled.

Austin turned red. "I never said that... oh, never mind. You have a favor to do me."

We turned to him. When it seemed like he figured out that we would do anything for the gem, he started talking again. "I need a present for my date..." Austin blushed. "I mean friend, who happens to be a girl. I can't find anything that would please her."

Zoe stepped forward. "I got this," she said. "What is her element?"

"Mechanics," Austin said nervously. Though it sounded more like a question.

"Mechanics plus precious metals..." muttered Zoe.

"Equals golden machines!" exclaimed Lily.

"Hey!" complained Austin.

Zoe glared at Lily. "I know what to do. But she won't want jewels. It's too common for you. That means she will want something unique. Something that you don't commonly have," she explained.

Austin smiled. "That was all I needed to know. Thanks!" he said, running off.

"Let's go to the next planet. We got this jewel," said Zoe, grinning.

We had to drag Moonstruck (almost literally) off the planet before she stole any jewels. Then we had to make her lead us to the next planet and not back around to this one, and she wouldn't do it, so

Silverstream did it instead, which got Moonstruck complaining the whole way there.

Then suddenly, she stopped. Her eyes gleamed as she stared at a giant bronze planet. The mechanics planet.

"Okay, let's go," I said as I started to walk forward. But Silverstream held my shoulder fast. Man, she had an iron grip.

I looked at her. "What is it?" I asked.

"Two words — security system," she said, pointing to a little floating plaque. I walked over to it.

"*Password Required,*" I read aloud. "Anyone know the password?" Zoe stepped forward.

"Since when did you know the password to the mechanics planet?" asked Kayla.

Zoe smiled. "I'm smart," she said.

"Uh oh," said Lily.

Zoe walked to the plaque and punched in some letters. Then she smiled and looked at us. "Come over here," she said. We walked over to her. On the plaque it read, *Password accepted.*

Then it made some squeaking sound. A small bucket of sunglasses emerged from the side of the plaque. Then the message on the screen changed to, *Please put these on immediately.* We did as it told us. After all, these guys were like, the best engineers, and anything that they told us to do, we should do.

A blinding light filled out as far as we could see. For a second, everything was muted. So quiet you could hear a piece of bread drop. Except that sound would be silenced, too. Also, we couldn't see. Probably the only thing that the glasses do would be to keep our eyes from burning out.

The light dimmed and gradually faded away until the lighting was normal again. The sound came back (although there wasn't much of it). I took the glasses off and looked around blinking. After I got over that, it seemed kind of stupid.

I felt frustrated. "What the (*beep*)? Nothing happened!" I nearly screamed. (P.S. The *beep* replaced something that you do NOT want to know about.)

Moonstruck rolled her eyes. "Something did happen dorkis. The protection spell around this planet broke. Some of these planets are smart like that," she said.

I felt my face get hot. "Oh," I murmured.

Zoe stood there, shuffling her feet. Kayla fidgeted with her rock (that for some reason she still had, obviously). Ashley sat down. Lily's eyes darted back and forth around everybody. Silverstream gave us an amused smile.

I made eye contact with her. "What?" I demanded.

Silverstream wiped her right eye. "Nothing. Shall we go?"

We walked across the bronze (sometimes rusty) floor of the planet. I could hear gears clinking from every direction. Suddenly Ashley stopped walking and I almost bumped into her. "Look," she said, pointing strait ahead of us. My mouth dropped open.

I realized where all of the clinking had come from. I was awed. I had never seen so many Magics in the whole time that I knew that they were real. In front of us were about one hundred Magics, probably more. They were all covered in soot and oil stains, but they looked like they were having fun and this was something that they did every day.

The machines were amazing, too. Every single Magic was inventing, upgrading, or copying machines. There was a boy who looked like he was making a hovercraft, which unexpectedly (for me) blew up in his face. But he just smiled and kept working on it.

There was a girl who was working on... *Was that a portal?* She had a big floating ring on one side of her, and another one on the other side. Then she stepped back and took out a remote (that looked like an Xbox controller), and pressed three buttons on it.

Glowing purple circley things appeared in the middle of the rings. The girl smiled and put her arm through one of them. I was surprised to see that it didn't come out the other side. Instead it came out of the other ring. She wiggled her fingers and smiled.

Suddenly there was a flash of purple light and a boom, which sent the girl flying backward. She landed. Then she got up, dusted off her jeans, and looked at the portal like, *Really? Now?*

She must've noticed us gaping because she asked, "Can I help you?"

I felt embarrassed. "Um, no. What's your name?" I asked.

Her smile twisted. "I'm Rihanna. What's yours?"

We introduced ourselves. "I like your name," Zoe complimented.

Rihanna shrugged. "My parents named me that," she said. "But don't get me wrong, I have nothing to do with the singer," she warned.

We also told her about our quest. She stroked her chin thoughtfully. "Element jewel. We have one of those here. So, change of subject. Your elements are storm, earth times two, ice, fire, and universe times two." We nodded. "Powerful group you have here. Let's go find GearHeart."

I was puzzled. "GearHeart?" I asked.

Rihanna laughed. "Oh, yes. GearHeart is what we call our jewel." Then she glanced down at our pets, who had found their way out of our bags.

"You got cuties," Rihanna said as she tossed them each a treat. Thunder yapped appreciatively and munched up a little dog treat.

"Uh, so, you have the jewel?" I asked.

Rihanna smiled. "Yeah, and I'll give it to you, if you do me a favor," she said.

"Aww. Another favor?" Lily groaned.

Rihanna smiled brightly. "The favor is…" she began.

Then she paused for a dramatic moment (no idea what that was for). She smiled and said, "Let me give you one of my latest and greatest machines so we can keep in touch. I like you guys!" Ash licked her paw.

I stared. Seriously, this girl was crazier than Lily. "Okay. That's fine. I wanted to be able to keep in touch with someone else, too," I sighed. "Supposedly, you would be my first choice."

Rihanna clapped her hands together. "Great! Let me show you the way!"

CHAPTER SEVEN CRAZY

RIHANNA

It wasn't so long when we got to a small rusty shed. Obviously, it was rusty, like I said. I'm sorry. I tend to say things over again. Thunder trotted beside me, and the other animals followed.

Rihanna held up her hand in a gesture for us to wait there. Then she walked inside the shed, and came back with something in her hands. "I have something for you," she said.

I tilted my head a little and slouched. "You can't. You barely know us," I exclaimed.

Rihanna threw her hands up in the air. "Do you think I care?!" she said.

"Now to think about it, no. I don't think you care," I murmured.

Rihanna looked like she didn't hear me. Which was fine with me. She handed me a black watch.

"Press the button in the corner," she instructed. I did as told.

The clock whirred and both the little and big hand started spinning rapidly. Suddenly a surprisingly clear hologram sprang up from the center and created a mirror image of Rihanna. Every motion she made appeared on the hologram.

"So. Cool," murmured Lily. Rihanna's smile got brighter. (Was that even possible, considering that her smile was already big?)

"This way, you can contact me whenever you want! Or when you need my help. I'm good at fighting, and I can provide you with all of the machines that you need," she said.

I was left speechless. We had just met, and she was making an attempt to help us. I found my voice and cleared my throat.

"Wow. I can't believe it. Are you sure?" I asked. Then I was about to slap myself. Of *course* she was sure.

"Never mind. That is really cool," I said.

Rihanna smiled. "Thank you. And that isn't even the beginning. It does a lot of stuff that I can't remember..." she scratched her head. "Anyway, there's a lot of stuff that it can do. Like I said, I can't remember. But if you give me a call and tell me your request, then I think I will be able to remember." Rihanna scratched her head again.

"Thank you *so* much!" I said. "And the jewel?" Suddenly, Rihanna grabbed a light bulb that was lying somewhere on the ground and put it over her head like she had an idea. Then she took out her remote and pressed a button, and the light bulb went on.

See what I mean? Rihanna is CA-RA-ZY!

Anyway, after she put the light bulb down, she said, "Push the button on the top right corner!" I did as told. The watch made some clinking sounds, and a little pole came out of the watch. Then it sprang into a full sized container with a little topaz in the middle.

"GearHeart," said Rihanna proudly.

"Wow. That was WAY easier than like, all of the rest of the jewels that we had to find," snorted Kayla.

Rihanna nodded. "So, I don't want to shoo you away, but it's four o' clock and something always happens…." she said. "I hope you guys have a great quest! Call me!"

We said thank you and left, which didn't seem like a proper goodbye, but we had to go soon. Then we walked out into the universe. Soon, we stopped for a break and food.

"Rihanna was awesome," sighed Moonstruck. We nodded. I looked at Moonstruck.

"What is *the Crest?*" I asked.

Moonstruck looked at me. "Well, it's a design that appears on every universe type's forehead when you put all of the jewels together," she said.

I had to think about that before really knowing what it meant. I gazed around me at the universe. Snowy tried to nip at a star.

Then we started walking on our journey again, and I couldn't help but thinking about how we learned to be like this so quickly. I started out being scared out of my wits, to going on journeys on different planets, and fighting monsters. It seemed like it had gone too fast.

Suddenly we stopped. I didn't know why, but then I looked up and saw a planet. No, that's not what I saw. I saw something shapeless, that was morphing into something else every half a second. Thunder tilted his head.

What I saw was the Myth planet.

About the Author

Rena Marthaler is a fourth grader living in Portland, Oregon with her two dogs. She wrote *Magic: The Crest* during the 2013 National Novel Writing Month, as part of NaNoWriMo's Young Writers Program. *Magic: The Crest* is her first novel.

She welcomes your comments and inquiries about the novel at magicthecrest@gmail.com.

Magic: The Crest is available at Amazon.com, CreateSpace.com, and by contacting the author at magicthecrest@gmail.com.

Made in the USA
San Bernardino, CA
19 May 2014